The Berenstain Bears'®

# HOME SWEET TREE

Stan & Jan Berenstain

Reader's Digest Kids

Westport, Connecticut


Published by Reader's Digest Young Families, Inc. Printed in the U.S.A. 
ISBN: 0-89577-732-0

Hello, friends.
This way, please.
Just ahead,
just past these trees,
is our home,
our Home Sweet Tree.
Home sweet, home sweet,
Home Sweet Tree!

Our tree stands tall,
fine, fat, and round.
Its roots dig deep
into the ground.

Come on in!
Up we go!
There's a lot
for us to show!

Look! Look!
Over there!
*You* know him.
It's Papa Bear,
snoozing in
his easy chair.

Papa always
takes a snooze
while looking at
the TV news.

Look! Look!

Look in there!

*You* know her.

It's Mama Bear.

Our mom's a super
cookie maker,
a chocolate chip
cookie baker!

Yum! Yum!

Let's have some!

Join us, friends.
Come, and we
will all eat cookies
in our Home Sweet Tree.

Come! Come!
Come with me.
There's more to see
in our Home Sweet Tree!

Come and look.
Look if you dare.
The cellar
of our home's
down there.

The light we shine
will show the way
and chase the spooky
dark away.

This is the place
where we store
what we don't need
anymore.

Toys and things
that we've outgrown—
cradle, crib,
baby's bib,
bottles, blocks,
toy telephone.

D
L E
T I

Why keep these things
that we store—
things we don't need
anymore?

Well, Mama says
you don't know when
you just might need
these things again.

But there is much,
much more to see.
Come on, friends!
Follow me!

All the way
to the top of our tree,
our home sweet, home sweet,
Home Sweet Tree.

To the special
room I share
with my brother,
Brother Bear.

My things
are here.
My brother's things
are over there.

My closet's neat.

I must confess...

my brother's closet
is a mess!

You've seen our home
inside and out.
Home is what
we're all about.

Good-bye, friends!
Please come again.
But will you also
Tell us when…

When we can see
*your* Home Sweet Tree?
Home sweet, home sweet,
Home Sweet Tree!